A Match Made on

Vijaya Kapoor

www.draft2digital.com

Table of Contents

Preface

In a world where societal expectations often dictate the course of one's life, there exist individuals who dare to challenge the status quo. "A Match Made on My Terms" delves into the captivating journey of Nazneen, a Pakistani woman who dares to navigate the intricate landscape of arranged marriages with her own set of rules.

As we embark on this poignant tale, we witness Nazneen's struggle to reconcile her desire for independence and personal agency with the cultural traditions and expectations placed upon her.

Each time a new family arrives, she finds herself thrust into the role of a commodity, evaluated based on superficial criteria such as height, appearance, and cooking skills. Yet, Nazneen remains resolute in her quest for something more profound—a true connection built on intellect, ethics, and shared values.

Author Vijaya Kapoor skillfully captures the complexity of Nazneen's journey, presenting a multidimensional protagonist who grapples with conflicting emotions and societal pressures.

Through Kapoor's vivid storytelling, we are transported into the heart of Pakistani culture, where family dynamics, traditions, and community play pivotal roles in shaping the destiny of individuals.

"A Match Made on My Terms" is not merely a tale of love and romance, but a testament to the strength of one woman's spirit and her unwavering determination to carve her own path in a world that often tries to confine her. It is a celebration of empowerment, resilience, and the unyielding pursuit of personal happiness.

Join Nazneen as she navigates the turbulent waters of arranged marriages, challenging the norms, and ultimately discovering that sometimes, the most authentic connections are forged when we choose love on our own terms.

Prepare to be captivated by this stirring narrative that transcends cultural boundaries and speaks to the universal longing for autonomy, acceptance, and the pursuit of genuine love.

Chapter 1

Piercing Remarks

"You're 25 now and still single. What a shame!" the remark echoed with disdain and disappointment, as her ears absorbed the weight of society's judgment.

"What is it you want in a man? Should you exceed the 'right' age, you might end up with an older suitor. There's no point in dwelling on the past," another voice chimed in, its tone a blend of resignation and practicality.

"It's a matter pertaining to femininity, one that requires careful consideration," a third comment floated her way, emphasizing the need for caution.

These comments, like persistent ghosts, haunted the spaces she inhabited—the walls of her own home, the rooms of her relatives' houses, and even the conversations that unfolded within her humble abode when visitors came to call. Their collective impact weighed heavily on her, stirring a mixture of emotions within her soul.

Nazneen remained impervious to such comments. At the age of 25, being single in Pakistani society was often deemed a transgression for women. Yet, she had long grown accustomed to the disturbing remarks that had filled her ears for years. Fortunately, she had developed immunity to their sting.

Despite her family's persistent efforts to arrange a suitable match for her over the course of a few years, Nazneen had remained unlucky in finding a compatible partner. However, after enduring the relentless torment for three to four years, she had reached a point where the events unfolding around her no longer affected her. She had grown indifferent to the circumstances, finding solace in her newfound tranquility.

Indeed, appearances can often be deceiving. While Nazneen outwardly convinced herself that she was unfazed by the constant turmoil, deep down, an inner battle raged within her.

The weight of the situation slowly gnawed at her, plunging her into a relentless cycle of depression. With each passing day, her spirit withered, manifesting in a tempestuous temperament and a constant state of discontent. The façade of resilience she portrayed concealed the invisible turmoil that consumed her from within.

In the solace of late-night solitude, Nazneen's tears flowed freely, silently bearing witness to her inner turmoil.

Resigned to her circumstances, she grappled with a sense of defeat, a departure from the strength and boldness that defined her character.

Self-reproach echoed within her, as she despised her own vulnerability. "There is nothing more loathsome," she mused, "than being unable to reign in the torrent of emotions." The very notion of losing control over her feelings was anathema to her, fueling her frustration and self-condemnation.

Chapter 2

Family Pressure

"For the umpteenth time, he's a fine man, well-educated, and with a respectable job. You insisted on finding an educated suitor, and here he is pursuing his Masters and PhD. What more could you possibly desire?" Nazneen's mother scolded, her exasperation palpable as she reprimanded her daughter for rejecting yet another potential match from within the family.

In the intricate web of Pakistani family dynamics, Nazneen had made it clear that she sought a partner with a solid educational background. Such expectations were ingrained within the fabric of conjugal matters, where preferences and desires were voiced when discussing potential suitors.

Despite her family's persistent efforts to persuade Nazneen into marrying the familiar candidate who seemingly fulfilled her criteria, she found herself lacking any genuine affection for him.

In truth, she held no interest or attraction toward him whatsoever. However, conveying this sentiment to her family proved to be an arduous task, as words failed to capture the depth of her disinterest and the complexities of her emotions.

Nazneen's parents had their own distinct reasons for advocating her marriage to the familiar candidate. Her father, driven by a sense of protectiveness, harbored concerns about entrusting his daughter's future to an unknown man.

Meanwhile, her mother emphasized the significance of familial ties, deeming it crucial for Nazneen to wed someone from within their own kinship. Such sentiments were not uncommon in Pakistani parental expectations.

However, the prospect of marrying someone she held no genuine affection for posed a formidable dilemma for Nazneen. She possessed a clear understanding of her desires and knew that the proposed candidate did not align with them.

To compromise her own happiness and enter into a union devoid of love proved to be a decision fraught with difficulty and internal conflict.

"Why are you all pressuring me like this? I have clearly expressed my disinterest in marrying him, and that should be enough. How can you expect me to enter into a marriage with someone I have no affection for?" Nazneen's voice trembled with anger as she vehemently expressed her frustration and lashed out at her parents.

The weight of her emotions fueled her harsh replies, a reflection of her firm stance and refusal to compromise her own happiness.

Despite months of discussions and Nazneen's unwavering refusal, the topic of her potential marriage continued to linger in the air, refusing to fade away. She had repeatedly pleaded with her family members to cease bringing it up, yet her pleas fell on deaf ears.

With her patience worn thin, Nazneen found herself at her breaking point, her resolve tested to its limits. The persistent pressure had pushed her to the edge, leaving her with a sense of exhaustion and desperation.

"My dear, he genuinely admires you. He has expressed his desire to marry you personally. He is a good man, and his family holds a respectable position in our community. So, what exactly is the issue?" Her mother's persistent persuasion persisted, as she fervently endeavored to convince Nazneen of the suitor's merits.

She pulled out all the stops in her attempt to sway her daughter's decision, highlighting the candidate's favorable attributes and the advantageous match he presented.

Nazneen felt her heartache intensify within her, a silent cry echoing deep within her soul. Despite her parents' efforts, she sensed a fundamental lack of understanding about her true desires.

They failed to grasp the depth of her yearning for a connection that transcended mere suitability. While the proposed suitor may not have been a terrible person, he simply did not embody the qualities and compatibility she longed for in a life partner.

The weight of her decision weighed heavily upon her shoulders. It was her life, her future, and she yearned to choose a path that resonated with her own heart.

The pursuit of genuine happiness meant marrying someone she, at the very least, had an affection for—a connection that went beyond superficial considerations.

"What am I supposed to do if he likes me? I have clearly stated that I do not reciprocate those feelings. I fail to comprehend why you continue to push me against my will," Nazneen's voice quivered with a mix of frustration and vulnerability. She wasn't a rebellious or unruly girl by nature, but when it came to matters that dictated the course of her own life, she held a steadfast determination.

The prospect of compromising her happiness in such a significant way ignited a stubborn resolve within her, one that refused to yield to the pressures of societal expectations.

At times, the weight of her parents' desires bore down upon Nazneen, tempting her to surrender to their wishes, for that was the pattern she had followed for 25 long years. Yet, when it came to the sacred institution of marriage, she couldn't bear the thought of settling for someone without genuine interest and connection.

The fear of entering into a union that lacked passion and fulfillment loomed large within her. What if she succumbed to the pressure, only to find herself devoid of interest and happiness in the years to come?

The thought of such a risk was too great to bear, compelling her to stand firm in her resolve to marry someone who truly ignited her interest and captured her heart.

"My dear, tell me frankly if you like someone! You can tell us about him. We have no objection as long as the family and the individual are suitable for you," her mother expressed, her thoughts leading her to speculate that Nazneen's rejection of the proposed suitor might be due to someone already occupying her heart.

Unable to fathom any other reason for her daughter's resistance, her mother sought to assure Nazneen that they would be open to considering a match that aligned with her feelings and desires, as long as it met the necessary criteria of compatibility and suitability.

A strange mixture of emotions surged within Nazneen, finding the situation almost comical in its absurdity. The contrast between her previous inclination to cry and the sudden urge to burst into laughter created a bewildering whirlwind of emotions.

She found herself teetering on the edge of sanity, unsure whether to succumb to tears or let out a laugh that bubbled within her. The sheer confusion of the circumstances had driven her to the brink, blurring the lines between sorrow and mirth, leaving her feeling as though she was teetering on the verge of losing her grasp on reality.

Nazneen expressed her frustration, emphasizing that if there had been a man in her life, she wouldn't have remained single for such a long time. She made it clear that if she had wanted to marry someone, she would have shared it with others and taken that step a while ago.

Nazneen had previously declined the idea of marrying a specific person, and she pleaded with others not to bring up the topic again. She believed that there are numerous potential suitors out there and trusted that she would find someone who is right for her. She requested that her decision be respected.

With her final answer firmly delivered, Nazneen left the room, leaving her parents to surrender to her resolve. She was grateful that they eventually ceased their insistence, allowing her the space and freedom to pursue her own path towards finding love and happiness.

Chapter 3

Missed Picnic

Nazneen's peace was abruptly shattered as her mother burst into her room, bearing news of yet another family visitation scheduled for 6 o'clock that evening.

The constant cycle of receiving and entertaining potential marriage proposals had become a relentless intrusion, interrupting her attempts to find solace in other activities.

Each time she sought to distract herself, the arrival of a "new family" seeking to "see" her served as a stark reminder of the ongoing pressure and expectations placed upon her shoulders.

Despite the disappointment that swelled within her, Nazneen swiftly set aside her emerging negative emotions. With the sudden revelation from her mother, she realized her plans for an outing with friends had to be promptly canceled.

Pushing aside any lingering frustration, she focused on the task at hand and hastened to leave as soon as her van arrived, determined to fulfill her responsibilities and face the situation head-on.

Throughout the day at university, Nazneen immersed herself in the usual routines and antics of student life, finding solace and enjoyment in the company of her friends. However, as the topic of the canceled outing plan arose among her companions, her mood underwent a subtle shift.

A sudden flashback of the news she received earlier before leaving for university resurfaced in her mind, casting a shadow over her thoughts.

As her friends excitedly discussed the details of their intended destination and how to get there, Nazneen found herself withdrawn, silently listening to their conversation.

Her mind was preoccupied with the upcoming family visitation, creating a subtle detachment from the immediate discussions at hand.

"I'm really sorry, but I won't be able to attend this picnic. I have to attend a marriage proposal," Nazneen finally spoke up, revealing the reason for her sudden change in plans. However, her friends' response was far from positive.

"We made these plans days ago, dear. You should have informed them about your prior engagement," one of her friends expressed disappointment, highlighting the inconvenience caused by Nazneen's last-minute revelation.

As she was the backbone of their group, her absence was deeply felt and disliked by her companions, who had eagerly anticipated her presence on their outing.

"Please come with us, dear. We'll only be gone for an hour; they can wait a little longer," one of her friends urged, trying to convince Nazneen to join them. However, the gravity of the upcoming marriage proposal left her with no choice but to stick to her decision.

"I insist, go ahead without me. My transportation will be here soon, and I'll be heading home," Nazneen announced with a heavy heart, knowing how much she cherished outings with her friends.

Nevertheless, she understood that these kinds of situations were not uncommon in their all-girls group, where occasional sacrifices were made by each member for various reasons.

Chapter 4

A New Proposal

Nazneen returned home, prepared herself for the arrival of the guests, and patiently awaited their arrival. Her mother entered the room and provided her with instructions on how to conduct herself in the presence of the guests.

She was reminded to drape the dupatta (shawl) over her head, as per the customary practice for girls belonging to modest families. Additionally, she was to serve tea to the guests while adhering to the cultural customs and etiquettes that accompanied such occasions.

Although these instructions had become a familiar routine for Nazneen, her mother would invariably repeat them before each guest's arrival. Without any resistance or protest, she followed the guidance given to her, having grown accustomed to fulfilling these cultural expectations without questioning or voicing any dissent.

Nazneen gracefully received the guests, comprising of the prospective suitor, his mother, and his sister. She diligently served them tea and then took her place beside the guy's mother.

The conversation began, and Nazneen found herself subjected to a series of probing questions, some of which she found rather uncomfortable. "Do you possess cooking skills?" "What does your daily routine entail?"

Despite the inner turmoil, she answered each question with a polite smile, mastering the art of maintaining composure in such situations.

After spending a few minutes engaging with them, Nazneen politely excused herself and took her leave. The task had been executed flawlessly, showcasing her adeptness at navigating these social obligations.

Once the guests departed, Nazneen's mother and brother engaged in a familiar routine of discussing and analyzing the visiting family's background and credibility.

This customary practice occurred after every marriage proposal, signaling the beginning of the match-making process. Nazneen, however, remained on the periphery of these discussions, playing a passive role in the evaluation process.

Her involvement was limited to dressing appropriately, serving tea, and briefly interacting with the visiting family. The responsibility of determining the suitability of the match rested primarily with her mother and brother, while Nazneen's role remained confined to the initial social interaction.

As Nazneen shared the events of the previous day with her friend Rashida, the latter responded with a compliment. "You're so beautiful, my friend; you could have any man you desire. What is there to worry about?" Rashida's words echoed the sentiments often expressed by others, acknowledging Nazneen's striking beauty.

However, Nazneen remained skeptical of such stereotypical beliefs.

She didn't put her trust in societal notions that suggested good looks alone could secure a desirable partner. Being a practical-minded individual, she placed her faith in truths and facts, recognizing that genuine connections and compatibility went beyond superficial appearances.

Nazneen held a firm desire for a man who possessed intellect, strong morals, ethics, and a shared religious devotion. While she held her own religious beliefs, she chose to keep her thoughts and convictions to herself, avoiding imposing them on others.

Instead, she demonstrated her commitment to her faith through her actions and behavior. However, due to the mismatch between her personal ideals and societal expectations, the process of selecting a suitable partner from the pool of proposals she received became a daunting and overwhelming task for her.

The pursuit of finding a compatible match who aligned with her values became an intricate challenge she grappled with.

Nazneen had grown accustomed to the frequent influx of marriage proposal calls that her mother received. As she passed by her mother's room, she would overhear the repetitive recitation of her own bio-data, including details of her education, current activities, age, height, and complexion.

Initially, this repetitive ritual had caused irritation and frustration to bubble within her. However, as she heard it play out time and time again, it had become a mundane and expected occurrence, no longer able to stir the same level of annoyance.

Nevertheless, buried deep within her, a profound sense of sadness and despondency lingered. The constant repetition of her bio-data being recited, seemingly reducing her to a set of qualities and physical attributes, had taken its toll on her spirit.

While she appeared unaffected on the surface, the weight of the situation had silently chipped away at her emotional well-being.

Nazneen couldn't shake off the disheartening sensation of being objectified, feeling like a mere item on display for potential buyers. The scrutiny she endured mirrored the meticulous examination of a product, leaving her feeling stripped of her humanity.

Insecurities began to seep into her thoughts, casting doubts upon her height, complexion, and weight. Despite her practical mindset and intellectual understanding of societal expectations, her experiences had taken a toll on her, causing her mind and heart to surrender to the weight of it all.

The constant evaluation and self-doubt had taken root within her, eroding her confidence and impacting her perception of self-worth.

Chapter 5

Thoughts and Dreams

After enduring twelve formal marriage proposals over the course of four years, Nazneen's patience had reached its breaking point. The cumulative experience had left her feeling disillusioned and grumpy.

Frustrated with the continuous cycle of evaluations and the societal pressure to find a suitable match, she made a firm decision: she would no longer entertain any more suitors, regardless of their qualities.

Instead, she charted a new course for herself. Determined to embrace a life of independence, she resolved to remain single indefinitely. Her revised plan involved adopting a precious baby and finding solace in the companionship of a feline friend.

It was a deliberate choice to prioritize her own happiness and well-being, free from the constraints and expectations of traditional marriage.

At the age of 25, while her peers seemed to be embracing motherhood, Nazneen found herself captivated by a different vision. As she observed her bank account, she couldn't help but yearn for the freedom to explore the world on her own terms.

The idea of embarking on solo adventures and remaining single went against the grain of traditional family expectations, which often placed restrictions on the mobility of women.

However, Nazneen firmly believed in her own abilities and dared to dream of a life beyond the conventional.

She allowed herself to indulge in the allure of these whimsical plans, envisioning herself traversing distant lands, experiencing diverse cultures, and forging her own path.

Though it may have seemed unrealistic within the confines of her traditional upbringing, she held steadfast in her belief that she could carve out a unique and fulfilling existence that aligned with her aspirations and desires.

As Nazneen approached the completion of her degree, she found herself grappling with a significant dilemma. Despite her initial resolution to remain single indefinitely, doubts and uncertainties began to creep into her mind. She acknowledged the intrinsic human desire for companionship and wondered if her decision to forsake a life partner was truly wise.

The longing for a partner to share life's joys and challenges was not lost on her. Deep down, she acknowledged her own yearning for a meaningful connection. However, the uncertainty of whether she would be able to find a partner who aligned with her values and aspirations loomed as a daunting question mark.

It was a complex and profound decision that weighed heavily on her mind, prompting her to question the feasibility of attaining the partnership she desired.

As Nazneen contemplated the prospect of a potential partner entering her life, a whirlwind of questions and concerns engulfed her. Would she indeed remain single forever, or would fate introduce someone into her journey?

The uncertainty left her pondering her next steps. Should she pursue a career and focus on her own aspirations, or should she wait to see what the future had in store for her?

The thought of merging her life with another person brought forth a mix of emotions. On one hand, she treasured her independence as a strong and self-reliant woman.

The idea of compromising her career or losing her autonomy felt suffocating. Yet, she also cherished the cultural aspects and the Eastern charm that resonated within her.

Striving to maintain a balance between her independence, cultural values, and religious beliefs was of paramount importance to her.

Navigating these complex thoughts and emotions, Nazneen found herself wrestling with the myriad of possibilities and the potential impact they could have on her life. The path ahead remained uncertain, requiring her to find a delicate equilibrium that would honor both her independence and her desire for companionship rooted in shared values.

In her heartfelt prayers to Allah, Nazneen pleaded for a partner who would genuinely respect and cherish her, or to be content with remaining single if such a person couldn't be found. She sought nothing less than the best, unwilling to settle for anything that fell short of her ideals.

This unwavering stance also manifested in her approach to relationships, as she refrained from engaging in temporary or superficial connections.

It wasn't that she lacked belief in love or a desire for companionship. On the contrary, she longed for a love that was permanent, genuine, and unblemished. However, finding such a pure form of love proved to be a challenging quest.

Navigating this struggle was a solitary journey for Nazneen, for she found that others often failed to comprehend the depth of her desires and aspirations.

People were quick to offer unsolicited opinions and judgments, highlighting the inherent challenges of dealing with societal expectations and the opinions of others. Yet, despite the external pressures and misunderstandings, Nazneen remained steadfast in her pursuit of a love that was both meaningful and lasting, undeterred by the complexities and challenges that lay ahead.

Chapter 6

Another Proposal Rejected

Within a few days, Nazneen received yet another distressing piece of news that shattered her tranquility. As she stepped into her home after a long day at the university, her mother dropped the bombshell of two additional marriage proposal appointments scheduled for the following day. The realization struck her like a nightmarish wave, engulfing her in a sense of overwhelming dread.

The already demanding task of attending to one family visitation in a day had now intensified into a daunting challenge of hosting two families consecutively.

Despite the mounting pressure, Nazneen accepted the news without a word of protest. She retreated silently to her room, seeking solace within the confines of her personal space.

The weight of the upcoming back-to-back guest receptions bore heavily upon her, a burden she carried with a sense of resignation, knowing that she had little choice but to fulfill the obligations set before her.

Each time she received such news, it cast a profound disturbance within her that rendered her unable to focus on anything else. The weight of the upcoming meetings weighed heavily on her mind as her mother provided a brief overview of the two prospective suitors.

She couldn't help but imagine them as potential life partners, envisioning a future that felt unsettling and jarring. The process of visualizing and then discarding these thoughts took a toll on her, leaving her mentally drained.

As the clock struck 10 pm, Nazneen made a firm decision to put an end to her ruminations and seek respite in sleep. She recognized the futility of dwelling on these thoughts any longer, understanding that she needed rest to regain her strength and face the challenges that lay ahead.

With a heavy heart, she allowed her mind to be quiet, hoping that the solace of slumber would provide a temporary escape from the tumultuous emotions that plagued her.

With a heavy heart, Nazneen awoke to a flood of thoughts and uncertainties the next day, contemplating the course of action she should take.

As she opened her eyes, a plethora of questions inundated her mind. Should she reject the proposals immediately or give them careful consideration? Was she truly ready for marriage at this moment in her life? Would she be left with limited options, potentially marrying an older man if she chose to delay marriage in the future? The relentless barrage of questions left her head spinning, complicating her thought process and leaving her feeling mentally imbalanced.

After aimlessly spending hours lost in her thoughts, she reluctantly rose from her bed.

The weight of her indecision and lack of genuine interest cast a shadow over her as she prepared herself for the day ahead.

Each step in the process felt heavy and burdened with the weight of her conflicted emotions. With a heavy heart, she adorned herself in attire that reflected her inner turmoil, preparing to receive the family, all the while feeling detached and distant from the situation at hand.

Nazneen fulfilled her obligation by receiving the first family, consisting of the prospective groom, his mother, and his sister.

Positioned behind the groom's mother, she engaged in a brief interview, providing the necessary information before retreating back to her room. Meanwhile, her mother, sister, and brother took charge of entertaining the guests, allowing Nazneen to gather her thoughts.

Once the family departed, Nazneen's mother entered her room, seeking her opinion on the encounter. Faced with the reality that she did not feel a connection or attraction to the potential suitor, Nazneen honestly conveyed her thoughts, sharing her genuine perspective without hesitation or pretense.

"You're 25 now, and the ideal age for marriage has already passed," her mother admonished, expressing her frustration. "He's an educated and financially well-off prospect. I don't understand what more you want. If you continue with this attitude, you'll remain single forever." Such scolding from her mother was a familiar occurrence, one that Nazneen had grown accustomed to over time.

It may not have deeply troubled her, but it elicited a strong sense of dislike and aversion within her. She detested being reprimanded for her choices and preferences, feeling the weight of societal expectations and the pressure to conform.

Chapter 7

Another Proposal Received

Following a two-hour interval, the second family arrived, but this time the prospective groom himself was absent, residing in a foreign country. Nazneen dutifully followed the familiar procedure, engaging in the customary exchange before retreating back to the sanctuary of her room.

Once again, the routine played out, and after the family's departure, discussions ensued regarding the potential implications and possibilities tied to this encounter.

As the final echoes of their visit faded away, Nazneen experienced a surge of relief.

With the responsibilities of the day behind her, she felt a newfound sense of freedom, liberated to pursue her own desires and embrace the activities that resonated with her soul.

Seeking solace and a respite from the recent experiences, Nazneen opened her laptop and downloaded a movie, immersing herself in its storyline as a means to escape her thoughts.

Halfway through the film, a sudden thirst compelled her to step outside her room to quench it with a glass of water. It was during this brief interlude that she unwittingly found herself passing by her mother's room, where she overheard her engaged in a conversation over the phone.

Intrigued by the snippets of conversation that reached her ears, curiosity prompted Nazneen to linger and discreetly eavesdrop, hoping to glean some insight into her mother's words.

"My daughter is 5'5, an average height girl. If your son prefers a taller girl, there's no issue. Perhaps you should consider another girl," Nazneen's mother conveyed to the person on the call. The words echoed in Nazneen's ears, causing a mixture of emotions to surge within her.

She couldn't help but feel a twinge of disappointment upon realizing that her height might be a factor that some potential suitors considered important. The conversation confirmed that this particular match wasn't meant to be, and Nazneen silently acknowledged that it was time to let go and move forward.

An immediate realization washed over Nazneen as she connected the dots. The family her mother was speaking to on the phone was none other than the one that had just left, emphasizing their preference for a girl with a taller stature.

A surge of anger coursed through her veins, fueled by the injustice of the situation. She couldn't help but feel a sense of indignation, questioning why the family had even entertained the idea of considering her when they had such specific height requirements. The presence of this rage served as a testament to the frustration and disappointment she felt in the face of such superficial judgments.

Each time a family was contacted, they received detailed information about Nazneen, including her physical features. The repetitive nature of this process fueled her growing disdain for the entire concept of marriage. Filled with anger and frustration, she retreated to her room, forgetting her initial purpose of getting a glass of water.

The intensity of her emotions prevented tears from flowing, as her feelings transformed into a torrent of ranting and raving. In that moment, she made a resolute decision, declaring with firm determination that she would not succumb to the pressures of marriage.

Instead, she vowed to focus on earning money and embarking on a world tour with friends, firmly standing her ground against the traditional expectations placed upon her.

"My dear, please be ready at 9 o'clock today. Put on a beautiful dress and do some makeup. Another family has expressed interest in meeting you," her mother announced, entering her room just as Nazneen was attempting to regain her composure, adding to her frustration with the news she dreaded the most.

"Mom, I don't want to meet anyone today; I am tired. Can you tell them to come tomorrow? I have already dealt with two proposals today, please," Nazneen pleaded in a soft, subdued tone.

The mere thought of getting dressed once more and enduring the repetitive process weighed heavily on her, making her yearn for a break from the cycle of meetings and evaluations.

"They can't come tomorrow, dear. Their daughter is visiting from another city, and she will be leaving tomorrow," her mother explained in response.

Nazneen, despite her reluctance, refrained from protesting any further. As conflicted as she felt, a sense of understanding pervaded deep within her. She recognized the significance of marriage in her cultural context, and as such, she didn't want to prematurely close off her options.

Though she didn't have a favorable impression of the two previous suitors,

Nazneen chose to remain open-minded about the upcoming meeting.

A glimmer of hope flickered within her, prompting positive thoughts to surface from the depths of her being. Despite the considerable effort required, she summoned the strength to rise from her internal turmoil, ultimately getting dressed and preparing herself for the arrival of the new family.

Chapter 8

Final Answer

The family arrived, and to Nazneen's surprise, the prospective groom himself accompanied them. As she went through the familiar motions she had become adept at after numerous encounters, she couldn't help but steal glances at the guy.

Though the presence of her family members made it challenging to engage in a proper conversation or exchange direct looks, Nazneen understood the importance of observing him to make an informed decision.

In that brief moment of observation, she sensed an air of confidence and decency emanating from him. The way he carried himself spoke volumes about his character.

Respectfully refraining from overtly staring at her, he displayed a level of respect and courtesy that resonated with her. Despite the constraints imposed by the presence of her mother and brother in the room, Nazneen couldn't help but feel a surge of positive vibes, sensing that this encounter might hold greater promise than the previous ones.

The depth of Nazneen's perception was undeniable. The groom's confident demeanor shone through as he engaged in conversation with her father, brothers, and mother without any trace of hesitation. It was evident that his self-assuredness stemmed from a place of genuine respect and decency.

This observation left an indelible impression on Nazneen, reinforcing her initial positive impression of him. She recognized the significance of these qualities in a potential life partner, further fueling her curiosity and intrigue about this particular suitor.

Returning to her room, Nazneen was filled with a wave of positivity. When her brother inquired about the meeting, she expressed her contentment, stating that she had no objections to marrying this particular gentleman.

Details of his credentials and other relevant information were shared with her, and Nazneen found herself accepting them without reservation. Material wealth held no allure for her; her primary desire was to find someone who would truly respect and love her.

Drawing upon her observations of his decent personality, she fostered a growing sense of trust in the potential for a deep and meaningful connection with this individual.

Despite not being aware of the groom's financial status, Nazneen made a significant decision to potentially spend the rest of her life with him, contingent upon her family's agreement.

The family departed following the customary discussions that accompany a marriage proposal, leaving Nazneen's own family to gather and deliberate on the matter.

The ensuing conversation yielded a mix of positive and negative reviews, with her mother expressing unwavering optimism while her father and brothers harbored reservations.

The topic resurfaced periodically, yet Nazneen chose to remain on the sidelines, as the dynamics of such discussions were nothing new to her.

While she acknowledged her personal interest in this particular suitor, Nazneen refrained from delving too deeply into the matter until its finalization.

She deliberately brushed away any intrusive thoughts, diligently adhering to her established routine. Weeks passed, during which Nazneen maintained her composure and resisted the temptation to become overly involved, regardless of the underlying curiosity and intrigue that simmered within her.

As Nazneen's mind wandered during her pre-sleep musings, she contemplated the ongoing cycle of marriage proposals. She acknowledged that if everyone in her family agreed and approached her about the potential match, she would say yes. However, she found little purpose in dwelling excessively on the matter.

With a resigned mindset, she anticipated that things would ultimately reach a conclusion, likely resulting in rejection.

Exhausted by the continuous barrage of marriage proposals, Nazneen had lost interest even in acquiring the guy's picture.

The weariness had permeated her being, leaving her longing for a swift resolution to this process. Her primary focus had shifted from scrutinizing photographs and profiles to simply seeking a definitive outcome.

After weeks of deliberation and deliberation, Nazneen's mother entered her room one day, seeking her final approval.

"Dear, your father is inquiring about your definitive answer. We have decided to accept this proposal. Do you have any objections?" Her mother asked politely.

"No, Mom, I have no objections. You can proceed with finalizing this proposal. I am in favor of it," Nazneen responded, giving her ultimate approval.

As she made this decision, a mix of emotions surged within her. She experienced both happiness and a sense of sadness, knowing that embarking on this path would bring unknown challenges.

The bittersweet sensation that enveloped her was both gratifying and complex. Nevertheless, she resolved to embrace the journey ahead, fully aware that she had committed to seeing it through.

Chapter 9

She Agreed

The following day, Nazneen's mother informed her that the groom's family would be visiting their home. Nazneen obediently dressed in preparation for the occasion, following her mother's instructions. When the groom's family arrived, they brought with them sweets and delightful treats, symbolizing the official beginning of the union between the two families.

The atmosphere was filled with joy and happiness, a surprising turn of events for Nazneen. She had not anticipated that things would progress so swiftly. Initially assuming it would be a mere discussion or casual gathering, she found herself amazed by the gravity of the occasion.

As pictures were taken and sweets were exchanged, an overwhelming sense of awe enveloped Nazneen, causing her to observe the event in silent admiration.

When Nazneen took her place beside the prospective groom's sister for the photograph, a question emerged from her lips, "Do you know your cell number?" The words made her extremely delighted.

In that fleeting moment, she instantly understood the reason behind her elation—it was a message from the groom himself, a message that resonated deeply within her. This unexpected gesture shattered her preconceived notions of the traditional and conservative nature of arranged marriages in the Eastern culture.

Instead, it had transformed into a thrilling and enchanting adventure, defying the norms she had come to expect. It was a delightful journey that exceeded her imagination, infusing her with a renewed sense of hope and excitement.

"Yes, I do," Nazneen replied politely, keeping her joy concealed beneath a calm exterior.

"Give it to me, please," the prospective groom's sister requested, and Nazneen willingly obliged, handing over her cell phone number.

Refreshments were served and pleasant conversations filled the air as the prospective groom's family enjoyed their time at Nazneen's home. The exchange of kind words and warm wishes created an atmosphere of joy and happiness.

Nazneen couldn't help but feel a sense of delight, even though she hadn't met the groom yet. The fact that her family and loved ones were celebrating this new chapter in her life brought her immense happiness.

It was truly a remarkable day, marking the end of the challenging period of meeting potential suitors. The thought that she had finally found her Mr. Right filled her with a mix of disbelief and overwhelming emotion. After all, she had convinced herself that she would remain single forever. This unexpected turn of events was both thrilling and surreal. Little did she know that this was just the beginning of an even more remarkable journey yet to unfold.

Chapter 10

The Call

Amidst the family gathering, Nazneen's heart skipped a beat as she opened the text message. The words on the screen ignited a sense of joy and excitement within her.

Finally, she had encountered someone who showed genuine interest in getting to know her. With a smile on her face, she responded to the message, expressing her current unavailability but assuring him that she would be in touch once she returned home.

In that moment, the family gathering lost its charm, and her focus shifted to the anticipation of their upcoming conversation.

She yearned to be back home, eager to delve deeper into this newfound connection that held so much promise.

She wasted no time in texting him as soon as she arrived home, and within minutes, her phone rang, signaling his call. As she answered, she couldn't help but feel a mix of excitement and nervousness.

"Assalam-o-alaikum," he greeted her formally, his voice warm and inviting.

"Walaikum assalam," Nazneen replied very politely, but there was curiosity and warmth in her voice.

"How are you?" he asked with genuine concern, his polite tone sending a pleasant shiver down Nazneen's spine.

"I am good, Alhamdulillah (Praise be to God). How about you?" she replied, her voice filled with genuine warmth and curiosity. With every word exchanged, her happiness seemed to grow, and she couldn't help but find his voice endearing.

"I am fine as well, thanks to the Grace of Allah," he responded, pausing momentarily before continuing with the conversation. He was aware of the importance of maintaining the flow of their interaction, eager to explore more about Nazneen and forge a connection between them.

"Are you happy with this decision?" he asked, his adorable tone captivating Nazneen's heart, causing her to feel a sense of vulnerability and excitement. She could sense a magical connection forming, as if their souls were resonating with each other.

"Yes, I am happy," she replied, her attempt to maintain a formal demeanor failing as her true emotions seeped through. She couldn't help but feel drawn to him, and the way he spoke only intensified her feelings.

"Are you certain?" he continued, his words casting a spell that intensified her fascination, drawing her further into his captivating presence.

"Yes, absolutely! My family has already given their approval. You don't have to worry," she reassured him, her words brimming with genuine sincerity. She felt a profound gratitude for his concern, understanding that he wanted to ensure her happiness and that her decision was not influenced by outside forces.

It was a meaningful gesture that deeply resonated with her, forming the basis for a solid and authentic relationship. A sense of thankfulness overwhelmed her as she silently expressed her gratitude to a higher power.

"Alright then, congratulations to you!" he responded, a sense of relief apparent in his voice. It was as if a weight had been lifted off his shoulders, knowing that her consent was genuine.

"Congratulations to you too," she reciprocated, sharing in his joy and looking forward to the journey that lay ahead.

"Are you happy?" she inquired, genuinely interested in his feelings. The conversation flowed smoothly between them, and she found herself instantly comfortable talking to him.

"Me? I've been eager for things to be finalized ever since I learned about you. I was away from the city when I received your picture and learned more about you. I immediately informed my family to be prepared for the meeting with your family upon my return. However, there were some minor issues that arose after the meeting. It did hurt me a little, but alhamdulillah (praise be to Allah), everything has been resolved now. I used to be one of the few single members in my family, but now, I can proudly say that I'm also on the 'taken' list," he added a touch of humor to the conversation.

Nazneen couldn't help but smile at his lighthearted comment, feeling a sense of connection and compatibility with him. The conversation continued to flow effortlessly, and she felt a growing sense of happiness and contentment.

Chapter 11

Dream Chapter

After about an hour, he called again. Nazneen couldn't help but fall for him as he spoke. His genuine personality and lack of ego won her over instantly.

It was a dream comes true for her to find someone with such a decent character who was genuinely interested in her. She felt her heart melting and her emotions flowing as they talked.

She didn't expect to fall in love during their first call, but she couldn't deny the romantic connection between them. It was a pleasant surprise to discover that such genuine and heartfelt interactions actually existed in the real world.

"What are you doing these days?" he asked after a brief silence. Nazneen was still reeling from their earlier conversation and snapped back to reality upon hearing his question.

"Just enjoying my last semester before university ends. I spend evenings at university and mornings at school. How about your job?" she replied, making an effort to maintain a composed demeanor.

"We're government employees, just going about our daily work. It's decent," he replied casually.

"What time do you leave in the morning?" she asked, feeling a growing sense of comfort and friendliness between them. Both of them seemed to have an easy-going nature, making the conversation flow smoothly.

"My dad and I go together these days at 7 am. Previously, I used to go alone on my bike. However, by the Grace of Allah, we have a car now, so we go together," he explained, providing her with a detailed response. Nazneen appreciated his openness and found his talkative nature endearing.

"I see. And when do you usually come back?" she inquired, keeping the conversation flowing. Despite feeling nervous, she found herself enjoying their interaction.

"Um... usually we leave around 5:30 and get home around 7, give or take," he responded nonchalantly. A brief pause followed, leaving both of them at a loss for another topic to discuss.

"Well, I should go now. Talk to you later," he said after a few seconds of silence. It seemed like a fitting conclusion to their initial conversation. They both ended the call and sat in silence for a few moments, processing the encounter.

Filled with a mixture of disbelief and joy, Nazneen's heart beat rapidly within her chest. The realization that love could exist in the real world overwhelmed her, dispelling any doubts she had about spending her life alone. She had found her ideal partner, the one she had always longed for, and it brought her immense happiness.

Overwhelmed with gratitude, she rose from her place and offered a prayer of thanks to Allah for this precious gift. She thanked Him for granting her a man who possessed honesty and humility, qualities she had always desired.

In her prayer, she also sought Allah's blessings to nurture and strengthen their relationship, hoping that their love would remain steadfast and harmonious. It was the beginning of a dreamlike chapter in her life, and she couldn't help but harbor a fear of anything that might jeopardize it in the future.

Chapter 12

Love and Commitment

He reached out to her the following evening and initiated a conversation about their daily routines. From there, their chats evolved into casual and enjoyable conversations, and Nazneen found herself admiring his friendly and approachable nature.

It felt as if they had known each other for years, even though it had only been a few days since they first connected. Nazneen was thrilled to discover that she had not only found a life partner but also a genuine friend, which had always been her deepest desire.

Unlike the stereotypical macho men prevalent in her society, he displayed a refreshing openness and honesty. He shared his thoughts, experiences, and aspirations with her, while also expressing genuine interest in her own life.

The foundation of their relationship was built on transparency and trust, with a shared belief in the importance of open communication. They vowed to embrace the roles of both lovers and friends, promising to support and understand each other unconditionally.

After a few weeks of preparations, they embarked on their journey together, exchanging vows of love and commitment. Their union was celebrated with joy and blessings, and they set forth on their shared path, dedicated to creating a life filled with happiness and harmony.

Nazneen sat in silence, reflecting on the incredible turn of events that had led her to this moment. It was beyond her imagination to think that she would find such a remarkable man after enduring the challenges of the matchmaking process.

It was a testament to her unwavering faith in Allah's plan, as she believed that He had orchestrated this beautiful union for her.

Gratitude filled her heart as she acknowledged that Allah had guided her out of the torturous period of matchmaking and blessed her with the best man in the world.

She marveled at the wisdom and providence of His plan, realizing that she had been led to this point for a reason. It was a humbling realization that reinforced her trust in Allah's divine wisdom.

September 9th, 2018 held a special place in her heart, for it was the day when their first conversation had sparked the flame of love within her. It marked the beginning of a journey filled with love, joy, and companionship.

In that moment of quiet reflection, Nazneen couldn't help but feel an overwhelming sense of happiness and contentment. She knew deep in her heart that she had found her soulmate, and she couldn't have asked for anything more.

With a heart full of gratitude and love, Nazneen embraced her new life, cherishing every precious moment shared with her beloved.

Together, they embarked on a journey of love, trust, and fulfillment, grateful for the beautiful gift that Allah had bestowed upon them.

In the realm of love, our tale unfolds,
A journey of hearts, a story untold.
From a world of doubts and swirling fears,
A love blossomed, wiping away all tears.

In the depths of fate's mysterious hand,
Two souls collided, as if planned.
With each passing day, their love grew,
A symphony of emotions, vibrant and true.

Through trials and tests, they stood side by side,

Facing life's storms, their love would abide.

In moments of joy and sorrow's embrace,

Their love shone brightly, an eternal grace.

In the moonlit nights and starry skies,

They found solace, as love's melody flies.

Hand in hand, they danced on life's stage,

Writing their love story, page by page.

Their laughter echoed in the summer breeze,

Their whispers carried on gentle seas.

In the warmth of their embrace, they found home,

A sanctuary of love, where hearts freely roam.

As seasons passed, their love remained strong,
An eternal flame, where hearts belong.
With every breath, they vowed to cherish,
A love that's boundless and will never perish.

And now, as we bid our novella adieu,
Know that their love will forever imbue,
Our hearts with hope, with dreams so grand,
For true love, against all odds, will always stand.

So let our hearts celebrate their love's refrain,
For it is love's triumph, a beautiful gain.
May their love inspire, ignite a flame anew,
In the depths of our souls, where love rings true.

And as the final curtain falls on their tale,

Let their love linger, an everlasting trail.

For in their union, we find a love so pure,

A love that will endure, forever secure.

–END–

Milton Keynes UK
Ingram Content Group UK Ltd.
UKHW040633310723
426074UK00001B/231

9 798223 573036